TREASURE ISLAND

Library of Congress Cataloging-in-Publication Data

Hitchner, Earle.
   Treasure Island.

   (Troll illustrated classics)
   Summary: While going through the possessions of a
deceased guest who owed them money, the mistress of
the inn and her son find a treasure map that leads
them to a pirate's fortune.
   [1. Buried treasure—Fiction. 2. Pirates—
Fiction. 3. Adventure and adventurers—Fiction]
I. Stevenson, Robert Louis, 1850-1894. Treasure Island.
II. De John, Marie, ill. III. Title.
PZ7.H6296Tr   1990   [Fic]   89-20561
ISBN 0-8167-1877-6 (lib. bdg.)
ISBN 0-8167-1878-4 (pbk.)

TREASURE ISLAND

ROBERT LOUIS STEVENSON

Retold by
Earle Hitchner

Illustrated by
Marie DeJohn

Troll Associates

The old seaman who entered my father's inn, the Admiral Benbow, sent shivers through me. His clothing was ragged, and his hands were weathered and cracked. Across his face was a deep, ugly scar. Behind him he dragged an old sea chest on a small, wooden wagon. Billy Bones was his name, and the song he sang only increased my fear.

> *Fifteen men on the dead man's chest,*
> *Yo-ho-ho and a bottle of rum!*
> *Drink and the devil had done for the rest,*
> *Yo-ho-ho and a bottle of rum!*

He walked up to my father. "Do you get much company here, mate?" Bones asked, casting a wary eye about the inn.

"Not much," my father replied uneasily. He did not like the look of the man.

"Good," said Bones. "This is the place for me. I'm a plain sailor, I am. Rum and bacon and eggs are what I want and all I need." He threw down a few gold coins on the counter. "When these are used up, just let me know." Then he looked at me standing nearby. "What's your name, boy?"

"Jim, sir," I sputtered. "Jim Hawkins."

Bones merely grunted, then went up to his room, lugging the sea chest behind him.

Every day during his stay, Billy Bones went out on the cliffs of Black Hill Cove. He gazed out to sea through a brass telescope. When he returned to the inn, he always asked if any other sailors had come by. There was one in particular he told me to watch out for. "The seafaring man with one leg," Bones whispered in my ear. "Keep a sharp eye out for him especially, Jim."

I saw no one-legged sailor approach the Admiral Benbow. But two other sinister-looking visitors came for Bones. The first was a pale man named Black Dog. He was an old shipmate of Bones and was missing two fingers from his left hand. Black Dog and Bones talked quietly in the parlor. But neither the talk nor the quiet lasted long, for a few seconds later Black Dog burst out of the room. His shoulder was bleeding heavily. And chasing him with drawn sword was Bones, his eyes fired with hatred. Black Dog howled with pain as he ran out the door and down the road.

Bad luck struck the inn when Bones had a stroke and was confined to his bed upstairs. Then, my father suddenly took ill and died. Grief hung over the house like a dark veil.

It was a bitterly cold morning when my mother and I buried my father. It was also bitterly cold the next day when a blind beggar came tapping with a stick to the front door of the inn. Never in my life had I seen a more dreadful figure. And no sooner had I opened the door than he grabbed my arm.

"Take me to Bill Bones straight—or I'll break your arm!" he commanded.

I led the blind beggar upstairs to where Bones was lying in bed. The blind man took one of Bones' hands and placed something in it. Then, without another word, the beggar went out of the room, down the stairs, and out into the road, moving as fast as his legs would carry him.

Bones refused to show my mother or me what the blind man had handed him. But we soon found out, for only a few hours later Billy Bones died. On the floor beside his bed was a little round piece of paper. One side was completely black. The other side had these words scrawled on it: "You have until ten tonight." I looked up at the clock, which just then chimed six times. Only four hours remained!

My mother and I realized that Black Dog, the beggar, and who knows who else would be coming back at ten. We had to be far away from the inn by then if we valued our lives. Then my mother caught sight of the old sea chest by Bones' bed.

"Quick, Jim. See if he has a key for the chest here. He owes us back rent, and I aim to collect just that and not a penny more."

I saw a string around Bones' neck. At the bottom of it dangled a key. I gave it to my mother, who opened the chest. Inside it were sticks of tobacco, two pistols, a piece of silver, an old watch, and some trinkets of little worth. Searching the bottom of the chest, my mother touched a canvas bag that jingled with coins and also a bundle tied up in oilcloth. She pulled them out and began removing from the bag the rent she was owed.

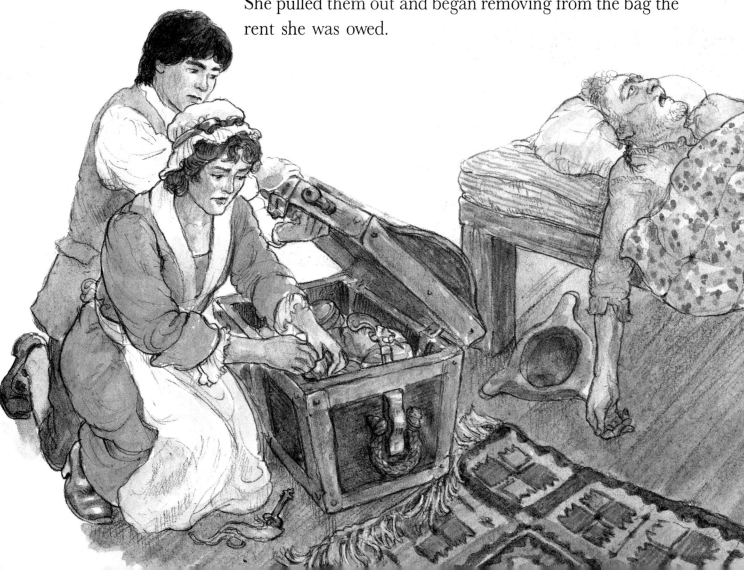

Suddenly, a tap-tap-tapping could be heard outside on the road. It was drawing closer and closer to the inn. We were both afraid now. Then we heard the sound of someone trying to open the inn door, which was bolted from the inside. A moment passed, then the tapping started again, growing fainter in the distance. Whoever was there, I feared, would be back soon enough with the others. We had no time to lose.

"Let's go, Mother," I said in panic. I grabbed the oilcloth bundle. "I'll take this to make up the difference."

We left not a second too soon. Behind us we could hear the shattering of the front door and the curses and shouts of the intruders.

10

Leaving my mother in safety a good distance away from the Admiral Benbow, I headed directly for the house of Doctor Livesey. This physician was also the magistrate of Black Hill Cove. I felt he would know what to do.

When I arrived at his house, a servant told me that the doctor had gone up to Squire Trelawney's estate. Walking in the direction the servant pointed me, I soon came to the squire's front door. A servant let me in, and I told both the squire and the doctor my story. I also produced the bundle I had taken from the sea chest of Billy Bones.

''With your permission, Jim,'' said the doctor, ''we'll open the packet.'' I nodded, and Doctor Livesey cut the thread holding the bundle together. It contained a book and a sealed paper. The book was a pirate's record made over twenty years. It added up to an enormous amount of gold.

''Let's see the other,'' said the doctor, taking hold of the sealed paper. He slit open the end seals and unfolded the paper with great care. It was a map! On it was drawn an island, with latitude and longitude and the names of hills and bays and inlets carefully inked. The map's markings showed that the island was nine miles long and five miles wide, with a hill labeled THE SPYGLASS in the center. And handwritten near a red cross on that hill were these words: ''Bulk of treasure here. J.F.''

"Flint!" exclaimed Squire Trelawney. "Those must be his initials. And this must be where he buried his entire treasure!" The squire then told us about Flint, a murderous pirate captain who had looted and plundered and amassed a great fortune on the seven seas. The whereabouts of this treasure were unknown—until now.

"The men who broke into the inn, Jim, were obviously after this map," continued the squire. He looked at Doctor Livesey, then at me and his three servants. "Gentlemen, let us all vow to keep this a secret. Not a word to anyone." The squire paused, then spoke again. "I propose we outfit a ship, hire a captain and crew, and go after Captain Flint's treasure ourselves!"

T wo weeks later, we set sail on the *Hispaniola,* the ship Squire Trelawney had bought for the voyage. I would work as a cabin boy during the voyage. The squire had made it possible for me to go by generously paying for the repairs of the Admiral Benbow. The intruders had left it in ruins. He even paid for another boy to take my place and help my mother with the inn.

Squire Trelawney had also hired the crew himself, relying on the advice of a sailor he'd taken on as ship's cook. His name was Long John Silver. He had no left leg, and under his left shoulder he carried a crutch. Perched on his other shoulder was a parrot, who was constantly squawking, ''Pieces of eight! Pieces of eight!''

Never have I seen a man of more cheerful spirits, whistling as he moved about on his crutch, eager to help out wherever he could. Most of the crew members who signed on were former shipmates of Silver. They seemed to look on him as their leader.

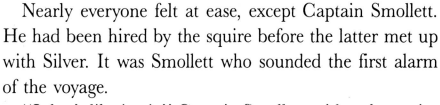

Nearly everyone felt at ease, except Captain Smollett. He had been hired by the squire before the latter met up with Silver. It was Smollett who sounded the first alarm of the voyage.

"I don't like it, sir," Captain Smollett said to the squire in the privacy of his cabin. Doctor Livesey and I were also present. "The men have little discipline and take orders slowly. There's also too much rum being drunk off duty. And I've overheard the men whispering about a map you have, with an island drawn on it and marked with the location of buried treasure."

Both Squire Trelawney and Doctor Livesey looked shocked. A blush of red came to the squire's face, and I knew immediately that he must have blurted out the secret when he was back in port.

"Do you fear a mutiny, Captain?" asked the doctor.

"I'm not saying that, sir. What I am saying is that we take a few simple precautions. And the first is to move the guns and powder on the ship to where the crew can't get them so easily."

"So be it," said the squire. "Order them moved."

At that, Captain Smollett went up on deck and commanded the crew to move the munitions from the forehold to right under the cabin.

The next few days passed calmly. But late one night, after finishing my work, I got a craving for an apple. They were kept in a huge barrel on deck. Because the barrel was nearly empty, I slipped my whole body into it, searching the bottom for an apple in the dark. Suddenly, I heard voices just outside. It was Long John Silver and his shipmates, and what I heard terrified me.

"Ah, mates, so far, so good," said Silver. There was a chilling directness to his voice that I had not heard before. "Just work hard, speak soft, and keep sober until I give the word."

"When might that be, Long John?" piped up a sailor. "I've had about as much as I can take from Captain Smollett."

"When?" cried Silver angrily. "By the powers, when I *tell* you. The last moment I can manage, that's when. We'll wait until the squire and doctor find the treasure for us and help us get it on board. Then we'll finish the lot off! One thing, though, mates. I claim Trelawney. I'll wring his calf's head off his body with my own two hands!" With that, Silver and his men shuffled off.

I was determined to speak to the doctor, the squire, and the captain about this matter as soon as possible. But then the lookout shouted, "Land ho!" A great rush of feet scampered across the deck to the railings. I climbed out of the barrel and made my way forward until I could see in the just breaking sunlight two low hills and a third, taller hill rising behind them. Treasure Island lay before us!

With all the excitement on deck, I managed to slip below unobserved and tell Doctor Livesey, Squire Trelawney, and Captain Smollett what I had overheard in the apple barrel. It was the captain who replied first.

"We have no choice," he said. "We must go on. If we turned back now, they'd mutiny at once. It'll come to blows sooner or later. But we have the advantage of surprise and some time. Can we count on your servants, Squire Trelawney, as being honest?"

"As honest as I am," answered the squire.

"Three," reckoned the captain aloud, "and ourselves make seven, including young Hawkins here. I'm unsure whether any faithful hands remain among the crew."

He didn't have to say anything more. We all knew what our chances were. Of the twenty-six people on board, it was seven against nineteen!

Captain Smollett ordered two boats lowered from the ship. They would carry Silver and thirteen crew members ashore. The other five crew members were to stay behind with the rest of us. But just as one of the boats was about to push off, I decided to slip on board without being seen. I hid myself in the furled sails. Once the boat touched the sandy shore, I bolted from the sails and darted inland, running as fast as I could. Behind me I heard Silver calling, ''Jim! Jim!''

The island was thickly overgrown with plants and bushes and trees of all shapes and colors. I started circling back after a while, and soon I heard a familiar voice. I got down on my hands and knees, crawling closer to the sound. It was Silver, all right, standing amid the crew members. His talk, though, was interrupted by a loud scream.

''What was that?'' asked a startled crewman.

''That? Oh, I reckon that was Alan,'' said Silver, referring to one of the crew members. ''We can't have men we can't trust now, can we mates?''

A sailor named Tom stepped forward. ''Long you've been a mate of mine, Silver, but you're a mate of mine no more. Killed poor Alan, did you? Well then, kill me! I defy you!'' Tom turned his back and started walking toward the beach. He got no more than a few steps before Silver's crutch flew at his back and knocked him breathless to the ground. Then Silver killed him.

I crawled away from this bloody scene, then ran. I ran and ran until I was stopped by the sight of a dark and shaggy figure. Immediately I thought of cannibals. But whether it was cannibal or monkey or bear, I could not tell. For a moment, I did not know what to do. Before me lurked an unknown creature. Behind me were cold-blooded killers. Which way should I run? Then I remembered the pistol I had tucked in my belt before leaving the ship. I decided to make my stand here.

The creature slowly came closer, then dropped to its knees in front of me. Why, it was a man like myself! He was clothed in the tatters of an old ship's canvas.

"Who are you?" I asked.

"Ben Gunn," cried the man. "I'm poor Ben Gunn, I am, and I haven't spoken to another man these three years past."

"Three years!" I cried. "Were you shipwrecked?"

"Nay, mate," he said. "Marooned."

I had heard this word before. It was how buccaneers punished an offender, by leaving him behind on some desolate, isolated island.

Gunn then told me his story, how he was once a crew member on the infamous Captain Flint's ship, how Flint took six crew members ashore to bury his treasure and then returned alone to his ship. Billy Bones was first mate, and Long John Silver was quartermaster.

"So it was they who marooned you here," I said.

Ben Gunn sadly shook his head. "Nay, mate. I was marooned by another parcel of rogues on another ship. We sailed close by here, and I told 'em of Flint's treasure. Their eyes lit up, all right, and they came ashore. But they found nothing. So the blackguards left me here. And here I've been ever since."

His eyes misted as he said this. My heart went out to the poor fellow. But then, he snapped his fingers and hopped in the air.

"I'm rich!" shouted Gunn, giggling. "Rich beyond my wildest dreams!"

I thought he was stark raving mad, though I didn't say so.

"I have a boat," he continued. "Made it with my own two hands. I keep her under the white rock. Worse comes to worst, we might try her after dark— " Gunn's words were broken off by the thunder of a cannon shot.

"The fight's begun!" I cried. "Follow me!" I ran toward the beach with Ben right behind me.

Soon we could hear guns firing in the distance. The underbrush gave way to woods, and ahead of us I saw the ship's flag fluttering in the air—on top of a stockade!

Ben grabbed my arm. "Your friends are in there, sure enough."

"Far more likely it's the mutineers," I replied.

"Nay," he said. "If it were them, think they'd hoist the Union Jack instead of the Jolly Roger? No, those are the colors of your friends. And by the looks of it, they're getting the worst of the fighting, even behind the walls of the stockade ol' Captain Flint made years ago."

"That may be so," I said, taking leave of him. "But I must join my friends." Before I left, Gunn said something curious to me.

"All right, mate, you must do what you must do. But when ol' Ben Gunn here is wanted, you'll know where to find me. Now, good luck, lad!" And off he went, in the direction opposite my own.

I edged around the rear of the stockade and finally made my way to the back entrance. There I was greeted by my comrades: Squire Trelawney, Doctor Livesey, Captain Smollett, and two of the squire's servants. The third servant, Redruth, lay dead along a wall. A new man, Gray, was there fighting beside them.

I told them all about my adventures inland, especially about Ben Gunn. Then the doctor quickly told me what had happened to them since I left the *Hispaniola*. The captain, squire, and he decided to take their chances on shore rather than on the ship. They would not leave without me, he said. And so, Captain Smollett surprised the pirates still on board and held them at bay with a pair of pistols. As he did, a boat was quickly loaded with as much powder, musketry, and food as it could carry without capsizing.

Then, with crewman Gray joining them at the last moment, the captain, doctor, squire, and his three servants pushed off in the boat. The captain had disabled the ship's cannon before jumping onto the boat. But the pirates surprised them by producing another long gun they had hidden on board. These were the shots now exploding around the stockade, where my comrades had fled with the stores from the boat. The fighting had been fierce, and Redruth was the first to die. Four of the pirates had also been killed in the fighting, with at least three others wounded.

The situation was grim, and Captain Smollett knew it. He assigned each of us to a post inside the stockade. It was deathly quiet outside now, *too* quiet. "They're gearing up for an attack," the captain whispered. "Stay by your posts, and fire when fired upon."

Suddenly, bullets whistled around the stockade. Sand kicked up and rained down on us. Splinters of wood flew through the air. The air was thick with smoke and sweat as we fired back.

Then, a small band of pirates leapt from the cover of the surrounding woods and ran straight at the stockade. The squire and Gray fired at the onrushing pirates, killing two and causing another to flee backward. But four had penetrated our defenses and were upon us. They were firing at us through the same holes we were using to fire at them. We were like sitting ducks! Suddenly, one of them burst through the door, swooping down on the doctor with his cutlass.

"Out, lads, out!" cried Captain Smollett. "Fight 'em in the open! Use cutlasses!"

I snatched a sword from the pile, then dashed out the door into the sunlight. I saw the doctor outside chasing his assailant, giving him a great slash across the face.

"Round the house, men! Round the house!" shouted the captain now.

The change of tactics worked. It confused the pirates who were on top of us, splitting them up. When the fighting was done, three of them lay dead. The fourth scurried back to the safety of the woods.

"Quick," said the captain when the doctor returned to our side. "Back inside the stockade!"

It was there, once the smoke had cleared, that we saw the price we had paid for this latest victory. One of the squire's two remaining servants was shot through the head. The other had a crushed chest and a fractured skull. He would not live out the day. The captain was wounded as well, though not fatally.

The mutineers did not attack again that day. No doubt, like us, they were binding their wounds and deciding what to do next. The doctor treated Captain Smollett's wounds. With Squire Trelawney, the two talked about the next course of action. Gray and I sat out of earshot at the far end of the stockade.

Then, without warning, the doctor took up his hat and pistols, put the treasure map in his pocket, and set off briskly out the rear door and into the trees behind the stockade. Gray and I were thunderstruck.

"What in the name of Davy Jones is he doing?" exclaimed Gray. "Is he crazy?"

"No," I said, "I don't think so. If my guess is right, the good doctor is going off to find ol' Ben Gunn."

Hours passed and I grew restless. I decided to leave the stockade at the first opportunity.

My chance came when both Gray and Squire Trelawney were helping the captain with his bandages. Taking some biscuits with me, as well as two pistols, some powder, bullets, and my knife, I silently left the stockade. Once outside, I dashed for the thickest of the nearby trees. I felt bad about leaving only two able-bodied men to defend the stockade. But I had a plan I thought might save us all.

I retraced my path to where I first met Ben Gunn, then searched until I saw the white rock he mentioned. In a hollow beneath it, covered by animal skins and leaves, was Ben's boat. It had a small, crude, lopsided framework of wood covered in goat skin. A long, double-ended paddle made from a tree branch was what I would have to use to propel the boat in the water. I dragged the boat close to the beach, then waited until absolute darkness cloaked the island. I was determined to slip out to the *Hispaniola* and cut her adrift.

Steering Ben Gunn's rough-hewn boat was not easy, but I finally managed to bring it alongside the *Hispaniola*. In the glare from the ship, I could see the anchor's thick rope in the water. I took out my knife and cut it strand by strand until it was cut completely through. Then I paddled away from the ship's side.

The effort of paddling out and now back, however, was more strenuous than I foresaw. My arms and back ached, and my eyelids started to droop. I could feel fatigue creeping over my entire body. And soon the lapping of the ocean waves lulled me into sleep inside Ben's boat.

I had no idea how long I slept. But when I awoke, I could see the *Hispaniola* coming straight for me! She was moving oddly in the water, as if no one were at her helm. I leapt free of Ben's boat just in the nick of time. The bow of the *Hispaniola* came crashing down, shattering Ben's boat and sending it to the bottom. It was all I could do to catch hold of one of the *Hispaniola*'s trailing lines and haul myself up toward the deck.

Afraid even to breathe and perhaps give myself away, I climbed to a point where I could see the deck. No one stirred. The only two pirates I could see at all must have been left behind by the others to guard the ship. One was a fellow named Redcap, who was lying on his back, motionless. The other pirate was named Israel Hands. He was barely breathing. Hands was propped up against the bulwarks, and his face was as white as a candle. Splashes of dark blood were on the planks nearby. Whatever argument the two pirates had, ended in the death of one and the near-death of the other.

Cautiously, I approached Hands. The stab wound in his thigh was still bleeding. He moaned, then opened his glassy eyes. ''Much hurt?'' I asked him.

Hands almost barked his reply. ''Me luck's gone bad. But not as bad as that swab's over there,'' he said, his eyes darting toward the seaman he had killed. ''I reckon you'll be wanting to get ashore with this ship. S'pose we strike a deal. You give me food and drink, and a scarf or kerchief to tie my wound up, and I'll tell you how to sail this ship.''

It seemed there was some sense in what he said. And so we struck the bargain. Before long, he had me guiding the *Hispaniola* along the coast of Treasure Island. I headed it toward an inlet north of where the pirates had beached their boats. In return, I gave Hands a kerchief for the stab wound in his thigh. And the food and brandy I gave him visibly revived him. He sat straighter, spoke louder and clearer, and looked in every way a better man.

"Jim," he beckoned, his voice unusually friendly, "be a good lad and fetch ol' Hands here some of that wine from the hold. This brandy's a mite strong for me."

Not for a moment did I trust him, but I did as he asked. I walked loudly upon the steps leading down to the hold. Then I slipped off my shoes and tiptoed barefoot out the back door and off to the side of the deck. I could see Hands, but he couldn't see me. And what I saw made my blood run cold!

Hands had limped across the deck to where a coil of rope hung by the railing. Out of the coil he pulled a long knife. Then he hobbled back to his place by the bulwarks. I now knew Hands could move about on his wounded leg. He was armed, and he obviously meant to do away with me the first chance he got. I returned to the hold the same way I came, got a bottle of wine, and gave it to him as if nothing had happened.

The shores of a northern inlet loomed ahead. With Hands still directing me from his position by the bulwarks, I steered the *Hispaniola* into the inlet. This maneuver took all of my concentration. But in the corner of my eye I saw a shadow move. When I turned around, Hands was about to lunge at me with his knife!

We both cried out at the same time—I for my life, he to take it. Instinctively I sidestepped his lunge forward, and his head hit the tiller I was holding. This gave me time to draw out my pistols and fire. But neither one did. The seawater must have clogged them.

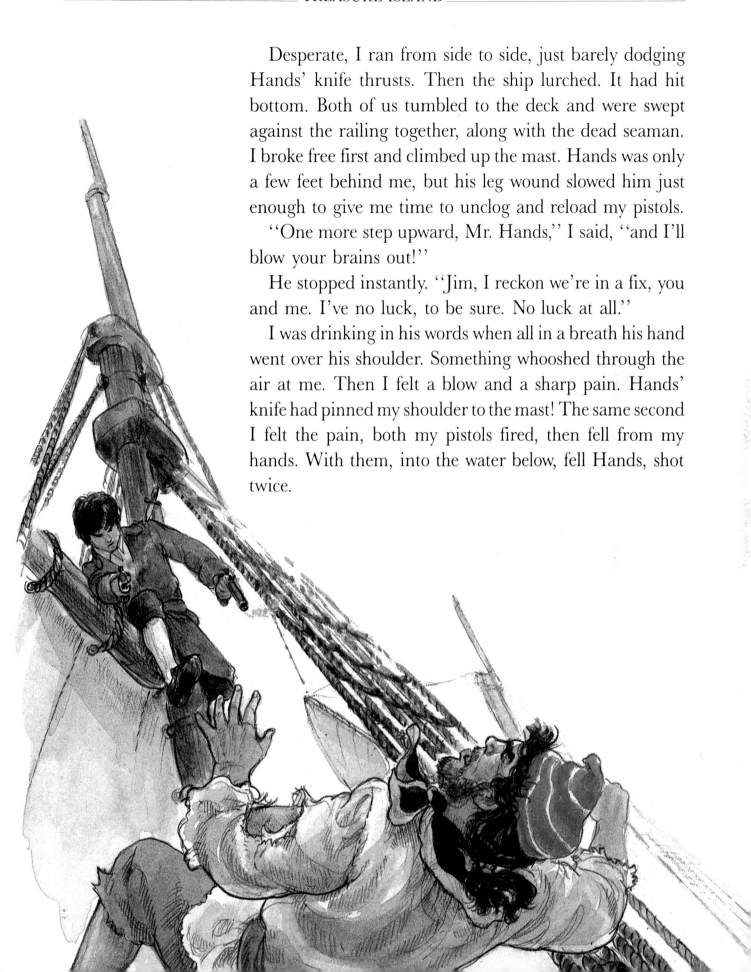

Desperate, I ran from side to side, just barely dodging Hands' knife thrusts. Then the ship lurched. It had hit bottom. Both of us tumbled to the deck and were swept against the railing together, along with the dead seaman. I broke free first and climbed up the mast. Hands was only a few feet behind me, but his leg wound slowed him just enough to give me time to unclog and reload my pistols.

"One more step upward, Mr. Hands," I said, "and I'll blow your brains out!"

He stopped instantly. "Jim, I reckon we're in a fix, you and me. I've no luck, to be sure. No luck at all."

I was drinking in his words when all in a breath his hand went over his shoulder. Something whooshed through the air at me. Then I felt a blow and a sharp pain. Hands' knife had pinned my shoulder to the mast! The same second I felt the pain, both my pistols fired, then fell from my hands. With them, into the water below, fell Hands, shot twice.

Blood ran down my shoulder as I carefully moved it free from the knife. Luckily, I had only been nicked. The wound looked worse than it was. I climbed down from the mast, dropped myself into the shallow water where the *Hispaniola* lay at an angle, and waded ashore. It was getting dark now. I set forth for the stockade and the companions I had left there.

Coming up on the rear of the stockade, I could hear the peaceful snoring of men inside. I wondered why no one was keeping watch. If Silver and his henchmen were to creep up on them, none would see daybreak. Still, I was happy to be with them again.

I opened the door and peered inside. Everything was pitch black. The snoring continued, and I heard a light pecking noise that I could not account for. With my arms held out before me, I walked slowly into the center of the stockade. My foot struck the leg of a sleeper, who groaned without waking. Then a shrill voice pierced the air.

''Pieces of eight! Pieces of eight!''

It was Silver's parrot! It was she whom I heard pecking before, and it was she who was keeping the watch! I turned and ran—straight into the arms of a pirate. After some further commotion, a torch was lit. The next voice I heard froze me to the spot.

''Well, well, well. If it isn't young Jim Hawkins! Come to drop in for a visit, eh? I take that right friendly, Jim. Yes, I do.'' It was Long John Silver himself. He and his brutal gang were in full possession of the stockade. No prisoners were in sight. As I looked about me, a pirate took out his knife and was about to slit my throat. But Silver pushed him away.

"Away, ye blackguard!" ordered Silver. "This here is our hostage, and I'll not have him killed. Understand?"

The pirates were confused. And in their confusion I summoned up enough courage to ask Silver where my friends were.

"Yesterday morning," said Silver, eyeing his men as he spoke, "down came your Doctor Livesey with a flag of truce. Says he, 'Cap'n Silver, you've no longer a ship to sail.' Well, maybe we took a bit too much rum and not looked out to sea as often as we should. 'Cause when we looked out, by thunder, the ship was gone! 'Well,' says the doctor, 'let's bargain.' And bargain we did. We got the drink and food and the whole blockhouse here. As for them, they've gone on their merry way, with no further trouble from us."

Silver stopped talking to reach into his coat. Then he flung something down on the floor of the stockade. It was the treasure map! Why the doctor had given it to him was more than I could fathom.

The mutineers pounced on the map like cats upon a mouse. It went from hand to hand. They were all giddy with the prospect of gold that was finally within their reach. And no doubt their sleep that night was full of golden dreams.

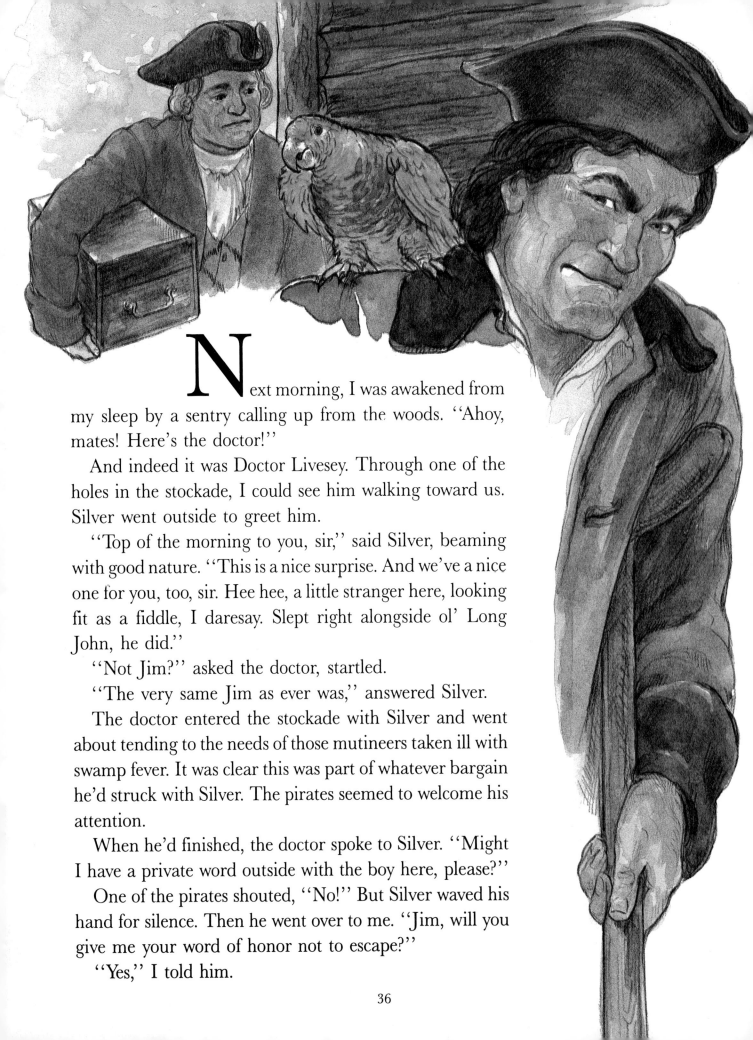

Next morning, I was awakened from my sleep by a sentry calling up from the woods. "Ahoy, mates! Here's the doctor!"

And indeed it was Doctor Livesey. Through one of the holes in the stockade, I could see him walking toward us. Silver went outside to greet him.

"Top of the morning to you, sir," said Silver, beaming with good nature. "This is a nice surprise. And we've a nice one for you, too, sir. Hee hee, a little stranger here, looking fit as a fiddle, I daresay. Slept right alongside ol' Long John, he did."

"Not Jim?" asked the doctor, startled.

"The very same Jim as ever was," answered Silver.

The doctor entered the stockade with Silver and went about tending to the needs of those mutineers taken ill with swamp fever. It was clear this was part of whatever bargain he'd struck with Silver. The pirates seemed to welcome his attention.

When he'd finished, the doctor spoke to Silver. "Might I have a private word outside with the boy here, please?"

One of the pirates shouted, "No!" But Silver waved his hand for silence. Then he went over to me. "Jim, will you give me your word of honor not to escape?"

"Yes," I told him.

"Then, doctor," said Silver, "you just step outside the stockade and wait by the edge of the woods. I'll bring young Hawkins along to you presently."

When the doctor left, anger erupted among the pirates. They accused Silver of doing what the enemy wanted. Only Silver's glowering stare kept the men in check. For the first time since I'd met him, I actually feared for *his* life.

Very deliberately, then, did the two of us walk down toward the wood's edge where the doctor awaited us. When we got there, Silver spoke in a hushed tone.

"You'll make a note of this, doctor," he said, "and the boy'll tell you how I saved his life inside the stockade. I know the ship's in safe harbor somewhere, and I know you didn't give me that treasure map 'less you wanted to. Play fair by me, doctor, as I've played fair by you and Jim here. I've no desire to swing from the gallows. Now, I'll step aside and leave you two alone." Silver moved off out of earshot.

"Jim, the woods are but a few yards away," whispered the doctor. "We'll make a run for it."

"Doctor," I said, "I gave my word of honor."

"I know, I know," he said. "But we can't help that now. C'mon, Jim. We'll run for it like antelopes."

"No," I replied. "Silver trusted me, I gave him my word, and I must go back. But before I do, you should know that it was I who took the *Hispaniola*. She lies beached in an inlet just north of here, below high water." I then told him of my adventures aboard the ship.

The doctor called Silver over. "I'll give you a piece of advice, Silver," said the doctor in a voice only we could hear. "Don't be in any great hurry after that treasure. And if you seek it, beware of trouble when you find it! I've no right to say more, for it's not my secret. One thing else, though: Keep Jim here close beside you at all times. When you need help, the two of you will get it. And if we all get out of this wolf trap alive, I promise I'll do my best to save you from the gallows, Silver. Goodbye, Jim." The doctor returned to the woods, while Silver and I started back to the stockade.

"I seen the doctor waving you to run for it, Jim," said Silver under his breath. "And I seen you say no as plain as hearing. That's one for you, Jim. We must stick close together, back to back, during this treasure hunt. We may yet save our necks despite fate and fortune."

Right after breakfast the following morning, with me walking beside him, Silver and his crew began the search for Flint's buried treasure. Silver held the map in his hand every step of the way, directing the men. We walked through thickets of green nutmeg trees and dense, flowering shrubs. The men were fanned out on either side of Silver in hopes of spotting the hill marked THE SPYGLASS on the map.

Suddenly, a bloodcurdling scream from a man on the far left stopped all of us in our tracks. Running over, we saw a large pine tree. At its base, entangled in vines, was a human skeleton!

"'Twas a seaman like ourselves," said one of the pirates. "Leastways, his clothing is sea cloth."

"Aye, mates," said Silver. "It's not likely you'd find any-one else here. But what sort of way is that for the bones to lie? 'Tain't natural, I say."

Silver was right. The skeleton stood perfectly straight against the tree, with its hands and feet held by the vines in an odd position.

"Take a reading off them bones," ordered Silver.

It was done, and sure enough the direction the bones pointed to was toward a distant clump of three trees on a hill. One tree was taller than the other two. "C'mon, lads," Silver said. "There's seven hundred thousand pounds of gold waiting for us."

Everyone quickened his step. But three quarters of the way to the hill, an old song came echoing out from the surrounding brush.

Fifteen men on the dead man's chest,
Yo-ho-ho and a bottle of rum!
Drink and the devil had done for the rest,
Yo-ho-ho and a bottle of rum!

I saw all the color drain from the men's cheeks. Even Silver struggled to stay calm.

"Flint!" cried one pirate. "It's Captain Flint's ghost, I tell you." The man dropped to the ground in fear.

"Ghost?" said Silver. "Nay, I never heard of any ghost speaking with an echo. And it wasn't Flint's voice, make no mistake. It sounded like, like . . . by the powers, Ben Gunn!"

"Aye, so it was," cried another mutineer. "Why, dead or alive, nobody ever minded ol' Ben Gunn!"

Their confidence restored, Silver and his men continued on. As they got closer and closer to the big tree, their terror was replaced by talk of treasure, of gold beyond their wildest dreams. The pace was even faster now, and soon we were all half-running toward the big tree ahead. Silver fell behind, trying to keep up on his crutch. When he finally caught up with the rest of us, we were all standing wide-mouthed in front of a huge hole. The gold had already been found, dug up, and taken!

Silver and I stood by as the pirates leapt into the hole. They clawed the bottom with their fingers. Meanwhile, Silver had slipped me one of his pistols. "Take it, Jim," he whispered, "and get ready for trouble."

The men climbed out of the hole on the other side. But for a two-guinea gold piece, no treasure was found. Their faces were full of hatred.

"This is your doing, Silver!" roared one of them. "You knew it all along!" But just as the speaker was about to fire at us from across the hole, three musket shots rang out. The pirate who had spoken fell face downward into the hole, and another fell dead on top of him. Seeing their two shipmates shot, the other mutineers turned and ran. It was then that the doctor, Gray, and Ben Gunn emerged from the woods with muskets smoking.

"Forward!" cried the doctor. "We must head them off at the boats." Soon, we were between them and the boats, and we all slowed our pace.

"So it's you, Ben Gunn, after all," said Silver, puffing from behind. "I might have known!"

When we came upon two boats left on shore, the doctor ordered Gray to destroy one. Then we all got into the other and headed to where I last left the *Hispaniola*. During the trip, Doctor Livesey told me what had taken place during my absence.

Two months before any of us set foot on the island, Ben Gunn had discovered the skeleton and then found and dug up Captain Flint's treasure. It took many trips carrying the gold on his back for Ben to get all of it safely stored in his cave on the island. The doctor had wormed this secret from him the day he took off from the stockade. It was then that Doctor Livesey decided to strike the bargain with Silver, giving him the now useless map and all the stockade's provisions. Ben had plenty of food and drink in his cave anyway, and there they could guard the gold.

44

As we passed along toward the inlet on the island's north shore, what should we meet but the *Hispaniola* cruising by herself! The last high tide must have lifted her off the sandy bottom, for she was now floating freely on the waves. Gray boarded her, fastened a new anchor, and stayed with the ship to guard her. The rest of us journeyed on to Ben Gunn's cave. There, we were greeted by Squire Trelawney.

When we entered the cave, we found Captain Smollett resting beside a fire. And in its flickering glow, I saw great heaps of gold coins and gold bars, doubloons and double guineas, of all sorts and sizes. Piles upon piles of treasure gleamed before us. And no one looked more amazed or happy than Long John Silver. It was Flint's treasure, all right, the one we had come for, the one that had cost the lives of far too many men.

After three days of packing, carrying, and stowing the gold on the *Hispaniola,* we set sail for home. On the shore behind us we had left as much food, drink, arms, medicine, tools, and clothing as we could spare. We knew the pirates who were still on the island would soon find them.

As we sailed around the island for the last time, we saw the pirates on a sandbar. They were begging us to return for them. It grieved our hearts to leave them in such a wretched state. But we could not risk another mutiny, and to take them home to hang seemed a cruel sort of kindness.

These were the thoughts crossing our minds when one of the pirates whipped his musket to his shoulder and fired at the ship. The shot whistled past Silver's ear and tore through the mainsail. After that, we kept under cover until the island was no longer in view.

We headed for the nearest port shown on the ship's sea charts. We arrived there one bright afternoon, and the bustle of people along the dock was more than we could resist. Leaving Ben and Silver to mind the ship, the rest of us went ashore. It was when we returned later that we found Ben Gunn alone on deck. Silver had gone—and not empty-handed. He had cut through a bulkhead and removed one of the sacks of coin worth a few hundred guineas. I think we were all pleased to be rid of him so cheaply.

We hired a few new hands from the port, then made good our cruise home. There, we parted company. All of us shared equally in the treasure, using it wisely or foolishly according to the nature of each man. Captain Smollett retired from the sea. Gray used his share to become part-owner of a fine ship. The squire and the doctor returned to their lives as before, and I returned to mine at the inn. Old Ben Gunn must have spent all the gold he received in the span of nineteen days, for on the twentieth he was out begging in the streets.

And what of Long John Silver? None of us ever heard of him again. But to this day, in the darkest of my nightmares, I can still hear the cackle of his parrot sounding the alarm. "Pieces of eight! Pieces of eight!"